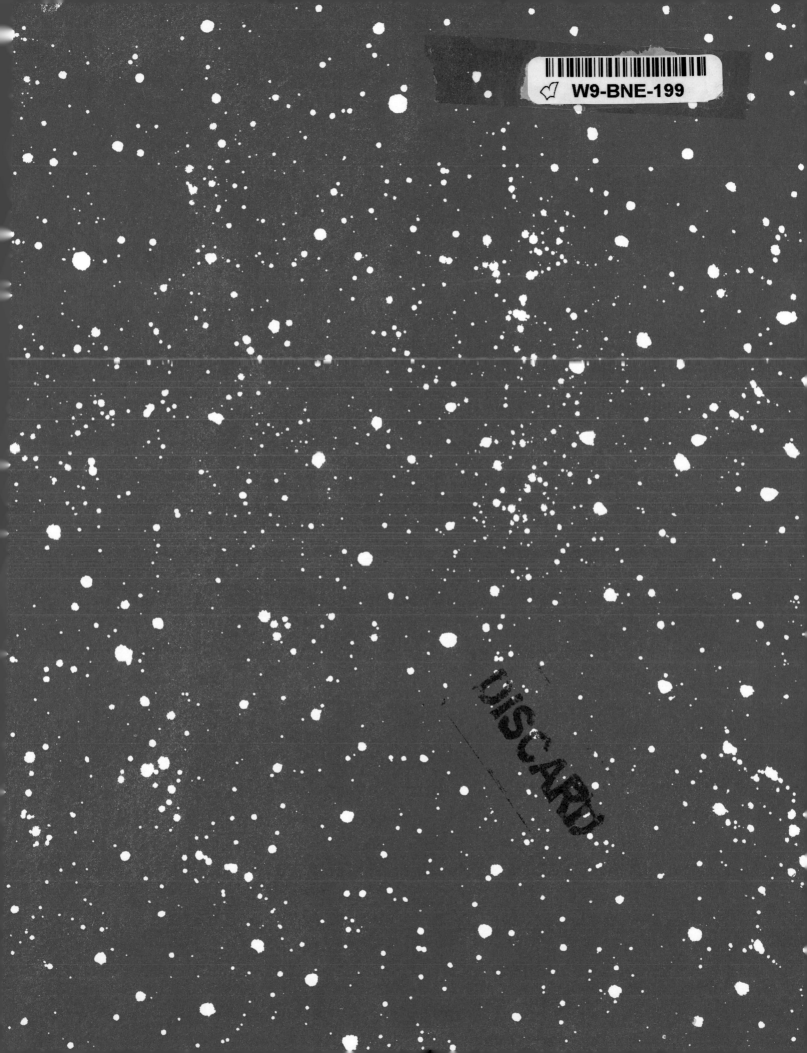

DADDY SPEAKS LOVE

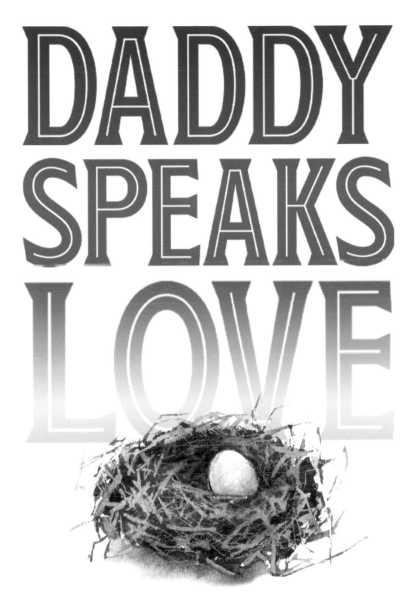

written by
LEAH HENDERSON

illustrated by
E.B. LEWIS

 Nancy Paulsen Books

NANCY PAULSEN BOOKS
An imprint of Penguin Random House LLC, New York

First published in the United States of America by Nancy Paulsen Books,
an imprint of Penguin Random House LLC, 2022

Visit us online at penguinrandomhouse.com

Library of Congress Cataloging-in-Publication Data
Names: Henderson, Leah, author. | Lewis, Earl B., illustrator.
Title: Daddy speaks love / Leah Henderson; illustrated by E. B. Lewis.
Description: New York: Nancy Paulsen Books, 2022. | Summary: "A tribute to the
joy and grounding that fathers bring to their children's lives"—Provided by publisher.
Identifiers: LCCN 2021017764 | ISBN 9780593354360 (hardcover) |
ISBN 9780593354384 (ebook) | ISBN 9780593354377 (ebook)
Subjects: CYAC: Fathers—Fiction. | Love—Fiction. | LCGFT: Picture books.
Classification: LCC PZ7.1.H462 Dad 2022 | DDC [E]—dc23
LC record available at https://lccn.loc.gov/2021017764

Manufactured in the USA

ISBN 9780593354360
1 3 5 7 9 10 8 6 4 2
PC

Design by Suki Boynton
Text set in Hertz Pro
The illustrations were done in watercolor.

*To my dad, who always speaks love
to so many, in so many ways*

−L.H.

*Dedicated to my first grandchild, Ava Rose,
and to all of the loving dads of the world*

−E.B.L.

On that very first day,
bundled in blankets,
you cried to be heard.
   "Shh, baby bird, I've got you,"
   are Daddy's first words.

Daddy speaks **LOVE**

when he answers endless questions

and makes a thousand plans.

New adventures await us morning till night.

Days full of tree climbs,

the longest of hikes,

of tea parties,
painted nails,
doing whatever we like.

Daddy speaks **TRUTH**,
not ignoring slips, spills, or scratches.
"They're part of life, little one.
Go ahead, make mistakes."

Daddy speaks **JOY**
in tickles and giggles.
Squishy hugs we share.

When Daddy speaks **COMFORT**,
I'm so glad he's here.
Shadows slip away
as he tucks me in tight.
Monsters will vanish as
he wishes me good night.

Daddy speaks **LEARNING**
when he says, "Listen up.
   This world isn't always fair.
   This world isn't always kind.
   And this you'll need to know."

He speaks what he's seen.
He speaks 'cause he must.

Daddy speaks **HEROES**
and the **DREAM** of a world that cares
that people of all colors
are treated fair.

For families to feel welcome,
to come to no harm.
He understands we all need
safety, protection, and space to belong.

Daddy speaks **FUTURE**
and of history's long, long past,

for Black lives to matter,
for compassion,
and change that will last.

Daddy speaks **UNITY**.
Daddy speaks **TRUST**.
When he says, "Equal,"
he demands it for each
and every one of us.

When Daddy speaks **PRIDE**,
he shouts it loud, his fist raised high,
his focus ahead.
Daddy will always speak out.

When *my* daddy speaks **LOVE**,
he teaches love too.
   "Speak your mind, baby bird,
   and remember—
   I've got you."

Now we speak **TOGETHER**.
Out in the world. Side by side.
His hand in mine.
    "Thank you, Daddy,
    for always being my guide."

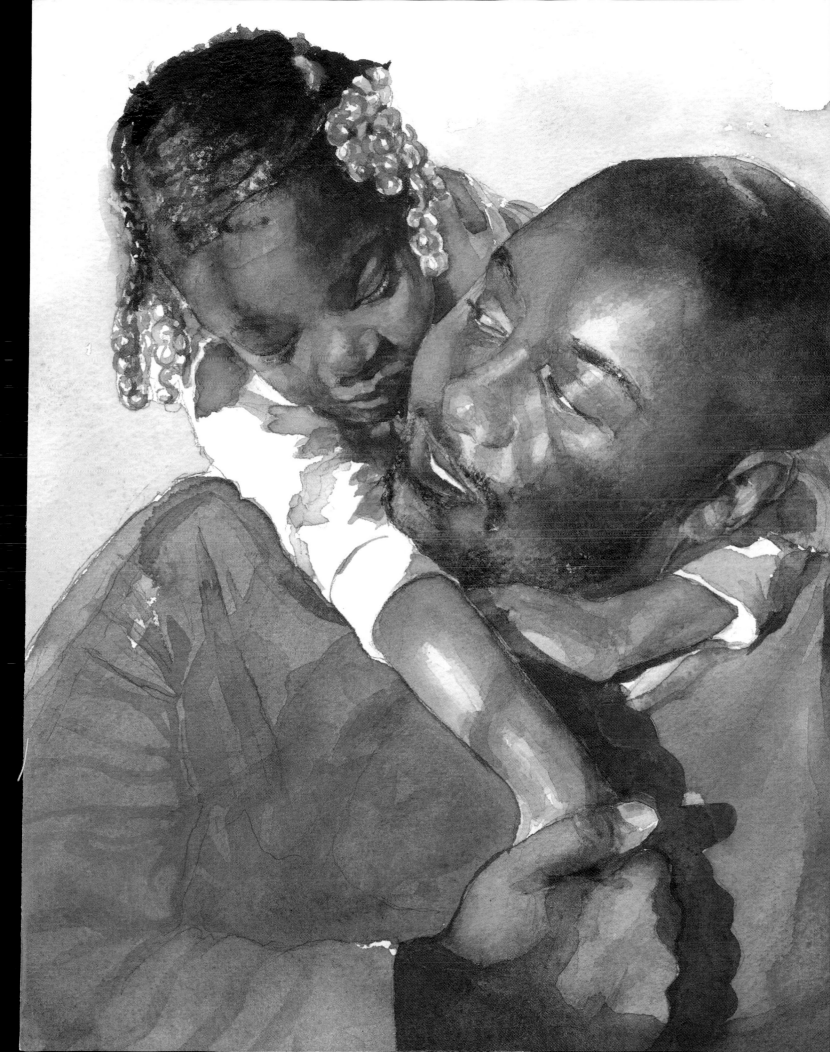

—AUTHOR'S NOTE—

While some books are steeped in research and others are created from a sense of needing to tell a particular story, this book poured straight from the center of our hearts.

We all bore witness to the terrible events surrounding the murder of George Floyd, and for nine minutes and twenty-nine seconds during our 2020 quarantine summer, the world's eyes were collectively focused on the senseless loss of a human life. The loss of a son, brother, uncle, and, most importantly to one, a father. Shaken and sickened by what transpired, it was the words of George Floyd's daughter Gianna Floyd that stirred something deep within another part of us. *Daddy changed the world* were not only words of truth, but words that encapsulated a six-year-old child's awareness of the lasting imprint her father's life would make—and they inspired us to explore the special bond a father and child share.

As a writer, my words mirrored the love-filled bond I have with my own father, who has always been a constant example and guide, and for E. B., his illustrations vividly capture the love he speaks in raising three strong Black sons. In creating this book, we also recognize the love, guidance, and support of those who occupy these spaces in a young person's life, and we honor and appreciate the role they play in helping to foster a more compassionate and just world. Our eternal hope in creating this book is that we may all find ways to speak love to each other each and every day.